PUPPY PALS

Murphy

Also by Susan Hughes

Bailey

Riley

PUPPY PALS

Murphy

SUSAN HUGHES

sourcebooks
jabberwocky

Published by Sourcebooks Jabberwocky, an imprint of Sourcebooks, Inc.
P.O. Box 4410, Naperville, Illinois 60567-4410
(630) 961-3900
Fax: (630) 961-2168
www.sourcebooks.com

Originally published as Murphy Helps Out in 2014 in Canada by Scholastic Canada Ltd.

Library of Congress Cataloging-in-Publication Data

Names: Hughes, Susan, 1960- author. | Murch, Jeanine Henderson, illustrator.
Title: Murphy / Susan Hughes ; illustrations by Jeanine Henderson Murch.
Other titles: Murphy helps out
Description: Naperville, Ilinois : Sourcebooks Jabberwocky, [2016] | Series:
  Puppy pals ; 3 | "Originally published as Murphy Helps Out in 2014 in
  Canada by Scholastic Canada Ltd." | Summary: Kat's new friend Grace and
  her best friend Maya learn to be friends, while the three girls help a
  lost cocker spaniel find her way back home.
Identifiers: LCCN 2015044673 | (13 : alk. paper)
Subjects: | CYAC: Dogs--Fiction. | Animals--Infancy--Fiction. |
  Friendship--Fiction.
Classification: LCC PZ7.H87396 Mu 2016 | DDC [E] 2 23 LC record available at https://
lccn.loc.gov/2015044673

Source of Production: Versa Press, East Peoria, Illinois, USA
Date of Production: September 2016
Run Number: 5007513

Printed and bound in the United States of America.
VP 10 9 8 7 6 5 4 3 2 1

For sweet Evany Logue

CHAPTER 1

uppies were scampering across the grass. There must have been over twenty of them! Some puppies were brown, some were black, and some were brown with white spots. Some puppies had perky ears, and some had floppy ears. Some had big, wide paws; some had little, dainty paws. All the puppies had sparkling eyes and wagging tails.

Kat was in her classroom, sitting at her desk. Her eyes were closed. She was having her favorite puppy daydream.

Her mother and father smile at her.

"Of course you can have a puppy, Kat," her mother says.

Her father sweeps out his arm. "Have any one you want!"

Kat smiles too. She looks at all the puppies, and she tries to choose. The little red Irish setter puppy gazing up at her with the dark-brown eyes? The black-and-white dalmatian puppy tumbling across the grass? The adorable wheaten terrier pup with the brown face and the black muzzle?

Suddenly the bell rang. School was over for the day, and the dream ended. But that was okay. Kat had puppy plans this afternoon.

"Let's go!" Kat said to Grace, who was at the desk next to hers. The girls jumped out of their seats, grabbed their things, and made a beeline for the classroom door. But before they reached it, they heard their teacher's voice.

"Katherine, Grace, where are you off to in such a hurry?" Ms. Mitchell stood at the front of the classroom. She was smiling.

Kat liked her fourth-grade teacher a lot. For one thing, Ms. Mitchell knew how much Kat loved puppies—and her teacher liked puppies too.

"You won't believe it, Ms. Mitchell!" said Kat. "Remember how I told you my aunt opened up a dog-grooming salon? We get to help her with a puppy today!"

Ms. Mitchell smiled. "How wonderful!"

"Her business is doing really well," explained Kat. "She thought it would take some time to get going, but she was swamped with customers all last week. So she asked Maya and me to help out after school. Did you know that Grace loves puppies, just like me?"

"I had an idea that she might," Ms. Mitchell confessed, her brown eyes sparkling.

Grace chimed in, "When Kat found out, she asked me to help out at Tails Up! too!"

Grace was new to the town of Orchard Valley. She was slim with brown eyes. Grace often wore her long red hair in braids. She reminded Kat of Anne of Green Gables.

It had taken a few days, but Kat and Grace had become friends. Not best friends, like Kat and Maya—they did almost everything together. Maya liked to tease Kat and make her laugh. She said, "You love puppies, but your name is Kat? That's crazy!" In return, Kat helped Maya with school projects and told her silly jokes. They had been in the same class since kindergarten, but not this year.

But now Kat had a new friend: Grace. And Maya had agreed to try to be friends with Grace too, even though the girls didn't know each other at all and they didn't seem to have much in common. Grace was quiet. Maya wasn't. Grace had trouble saying how she felt about things. Maya did not.

Kat was keeping her fingers crossed that her two friends—her best friend and her new friend—would get along. This was the first time they were going to hang out together. They were going to Tails Up! together, and Kat had invited both girls to come over for dinner after. Maya had been to Kat's house at least a million times, but it would be Grace's very first time.

"Well, how lovely!" Ms. Mitchell looked pleased. "Any puppy would be very lucky to have you three looking after him. Have fun, girls!"

Kat and Grace hurried out of the school and across the playground. They stopped to look for Maya. They were all walking to Tails Up! together.

"Sorry I'm late." Maya ran up, trying to catch her breath. "Okay, let's go. But just tell me one thing: did I miss the answer to the joke?"

"Oh, right, the joke!" Grace said, grinning. She rolled her eyes. Every morning, Kat told a joke. Today it was, "Why are dalmatians not good at hide-and-seek?" As usual, she made her friends wait forever before she told them the answer.

"So tell us, Kat-Nip," Maya demanded. "Answer."

"Are you sure?" Kat teased. "You don't want to guess again?"

"Oh, please. Put us out of our misery," Maya said. "Right, Grace?"

"Right!" Grace chimed in.

"Here goes: dalmatians aren't good at hide-and-seek because they're always spotted!" Kat said.

"Agh!" moaned Grace and Maya.

"Worst joke ever!" Maya complained happily, as they all rushed toward Tails Up!

CHAPTER 2

The waiting room was packed, just as it had been every afternoon since Tails Up! opened. Today, a red-haired woman sat with a perky Yorkshire terrier on her lap. Another woman was weighing her schnauzer on the doggy scale. A big man sat with a collie lying at his feet. The dog was panting nervously. Another man, thin and fidgety, sat alone on a chair. He wore black glasses. His long legs were crossed, and one foot was bouncing.

There was no one behind the front counter. Aunt Jenn hadn't hired a receptionist yet.

The girls stood along the wall, waiting patiently. Grace took a dog magazine from the rack and began reading. Maya elbowed Kat. She jerked her head toward the man sitting alone. "Greyhound. Totally," she whispered. It was one of the girls' favorite games. They saw a person and named the dog breed he or she most resembled.

Kat giggled and nodded. *Yes. A greyhound. Absolutely.*

A few minutes later, Aunt Jenn came out of the grooming room. She wore her pink grooming coat, and her brown hair was pulled back in a ponytail. She cuddled a skinny whippet in her arms.

"Oh, you sweet gal," she cooed to the dog. "Having those toenails clipped wasn't so bad, was it? You don't need to be so nervous next time."

She handed the dog to the skinny man.

Kat and Maya looked at each other and smiled. "Close!" Kat said to her friend. The man's dog wasn't a greyhound, but Maya hadn't been far off.

Grace looked puzzled. "Tell you later," Kat promised.

"Did it go all right? You're sure my Milly is fine?" the man asked, his nose twitching. Clutching Milly in one arm, he pushed at his glasses once, twice. His Adam's apple bobbed in his throat as he swallowed.

"Oh, yes." Aunt Jenn gave the man's arm a reassuring pat. "She calmed right down once I started."

"Yes. Yes. Of course." The man cleared his throat again. "Not sure why she gets so nervous about things. Well, thank you. Good-bye then."

Aunt Jenn greeted the three girls with a happy smile and waved them into her office. Inside there were two large grooming tables and two stand dryers. Along the walls were tables holding baskets of grooming brushes, clippers, shavers, shampoo bottles, and other equipment.

Aunt Jenn closed the door, sank down into her chair, and blew out a sigh.

"This is the first time I've sat down all day!" she said. "People have been dropping by with their dogs since I opened my door this morning. And the phone has been ringing off the hook!"

Just then, the phone out in the waiting room began ringing. "Isn't it great?" Aunt Jenn punched her fist in the air.

The girls laughed.

"So, Kitty-Kat," said Aunt Jenn, using her special name for Kat. "I'm relieved that you and your pals can help me out again this week. But are you sure you have enough time? I don't want your parents getting angry with me because you aren't doing your schoolwork!"

"We have lots of time," said Kat firmly. "We can be here every day after school this week. Right, Grace? Maya?"

"Right," Maya agreed.

Grace nodded. She pulled on the end of one of her braids.

"Wonderful. So, let me tell you about this week's puppy." Aunt Jenn popped a piece of gum in her mouth. "Murphy is a three-month-old Shetland sheepdog, or sheltie. Because they are sheepdogs, they have a bit of a herding instinct. That means they like to chase and, well, herd things. They aren't big dogs. They are friendly, loyal, and gentle. Murphy's owner, Brad, is away visiting his ill grandmother. He told me that Murphy needs lots of exercise. He likes to run and play." Aunt Jenn lifted her eyebrows. She blew a pink bubble with her gum. "So, what do you think, girls?"

"We'd love to walk him, Aunt Jenn," Kat said excitedly.

"Perfect," said Aunt Jenn, jumping up. "Let me introduce you!" Adjusting her hair into a new, neater ponytail, she led the way back into the waiting room.

The woman with the Yorkshire terrier stood up. "Are we next?" she asked. The Yorkie yipped.

"In a moment, Mrs. Potts and Pixie," said Aunt Jenn with a smile.

Mrs. Potts sat down, grumbling, and Pixie yipped again.

"Are you sure you wouldn't like to leave your dogs with me until I can get to them?" Aunt Jenn asked the two other customers with dogs. "Really, I have a nice big area where they can wait for their appointments."

The man with the collie shook his head. "No thanks. I prefer to wait."

"What about Max?" asked Aunt Jenn. The woman with the schnauzer glanced at her watch and agreed. She promised to return in two hours.

Aunt Jenn asked Maya to take Max's leash. Then they all went into the doggy day care room in the back. It was large, with four dog kennels in a row along one wall. There was also a large fenced-in area, like a playpen.

"That's where Max can go," Aunt Jenn said.

Maya led the dog into the pen and unclipped his leash. She stepped back out and closed the gate behind her. Max ran to the water bowl and drank. Then, wagging his tail, he sniffed around the edges of the fence, and finally lay down on the dog bed. In a moment he was asleep.

In the meantime, Kat had spotted Murphy. And Murphy had spotted them!

The girls and Aunt Jenn hurried over to his kennel to say hello.

"What a sweet little guy!" cooed Grace.

"He's adorable," said Kat.

The sheltie pup wagged his tail so hard, his whole body wiggled.

"His coat is such a beautiful color," said Maya.

"Yes," agreed Aunt Jenn. "And it will stay beautiful even as it changes. Sheltie coats start off light and they darken as the pups grow up."

Murphy was a lovely golden color, with a light covering of black on top. He had a white chest and collar. Each of his paws was tipped in white. His nose was black, his tail was black, and his eyes were dark brown. His ears were tipped down.

"Murphy! How are you, boy?" asked Kat. "What a sweetheart!"

Murphy wagged and wiggled some more.

"Now, like most shelties, this little guy might be a little shy with you girls. His owner said he takes his time to get to know people," Aunt Jenn said. She opened the door to the kennel. "Here, lift him out, Kat."

Carefully, Kat scooped up the puppy. Murphy squirmed happily in her arms. He poked his nose against Kat's face, then licked her cheek.

He smelled so lovely! Kat stroked his head and then scratched behind his ears.

"Okay, clearly a match made in heaven. Now

I must give a brush-and-cut to the very patient Pixie," Aunt Jenn joked. She blew another pink bubble with her gum. "Girls, I'll see you later."

Once the door was closed, Kat held Murphy for a few more minutes, breathing in his sweet puppy smell. Then, reluctantly, she set him down.

The excited puppy raced over to the fenced-in area where Max slept. Murphy wagged his tail, waiting for Max to wake up and play with him. But Max just yawned and didn't open his eyes.

Murphy wagged his tail again and then began exploring the room, sniffing the bags of dog food, the other kennels, and the closed door.

The girls watched, entranced. Then Maya said, "Hey, what about us, Murphy? We want to say hi too!" She crouched down and put out her hand. "Come here, boy!"

The sheltie pup stopped. He cocked his head inquisitively.

"Come on, boy!" Maya said encouragingly.

Hesitantly, Murphy began trotting toward her. But as he got close, he changed his mind. He veered away, toward Kat, but his paws slipped on the tiled floor. He skidded sideways, then scrambled back onto his feet, ran to Kat, and hid between her legs. Once safe, he peered out at Maya and Grace.

Maya burst out laughing and Grace smiled.

"You don't have to be shy of us," Grace said softly. "We're your friends."

Murphy gave his tail one small wag. The girls laughed again.

"I guess he's a little clingy to me because I was the first one of us to pick him up," said Kat.

She bent down and clipped the leash to

Murphy's collar. "Okay, tough guy," Kat said with a grin. "Time for the park!"

CHAPTER 3

The girls left the clinic through the back door. Kat was surprised that the puppy was so good on the leash. He didn't wander onto lawns to sniff trees. He didn't lie down in puddles. Instead he seemed to like staying close to Kat. He bounded along beside her, his nose up, his tail high.

Just being with Murphy gave Kat such a feeling of happiness. Looking at the adorable puppy made her smile!

As Kat walked ahead with the pup, she listened to Grace and Maya chatting behind her.

"I read that shelties are protective. They bark a lot to warn their family of intruders, unless they're trained not to," Maya said.

"Our farm dog, Bella, was a mutt," Grace said. "We never knew what breeds were in her, but we thought that there might have been a bit of sheltie. And maybe a dash of husky and a pinch of hound. We always joked that Bella was like a secret recipe!"

Maya didn't say anything for a moment. Then she said, "There are so many great dog breeds. I keep changing my mind about which one I like best." She yanked at Kat's hair. "It drives Kat-Nip crazy!"

25

Kat turned around, and Maya made a funny face at her.

"I'm not sure what my favorite breed is," Grace said. "We never even talked about getting a dog or what breed we wanted. Bella just showed up on our farm one day."

"Really?" asked Kat. She wanted to hear more about Bella, but Maya interrupted. "One week, I like pugs best," said Maya. It was like she hadn't even heard what Grace was saying. She went on, "Another week, I like rottweilers. This week, I would choose a...a Lhasa apso, I think. Do you know what those are?"

Grace began to answer, but Maya didn't give her a chance. "Lhasa apsos are small-ish dogs. They have beautiful long hair that sweeps along the ground when they walk.

They have long ears and long bangs. They are like one big hairdo!"

"Bella had long ears," said Grace. "Her hair was a mix of several colors: gold, white, black, and brown. What color are Lhasa apsos?"

"Lhasa apsos remind me of a doll I had when I was little," Maya continued. "She had hair that puffed out of the top of her head. You could pull on it, make it long, and then brush it or style it. Once, I even cut my doll's hair!"

That's weird, thought Kat. *Is Maya ignoring Grace? It's like she's having a conversation with herself!*

Maya moved up to walk beside Kat, leaving Grace behind. She linked arms with Kat. "Murphy is doing so well on the leash!" she said. "He's such a cute little guy. It will be so great to add him to our Puppy Collection!"

Kat felt awkward. Grace was being left out. And they hadn't really told her about the Puppy Collection. It was a special scrapbook they were creating. Kat and Maya drew pictures and wrote about each breed of puppy that they liked. They were going to include all the puppies they helped look after at Tails Up! too.

Why had Maya mentioned the scrapbook? Kat wondered miserably. Was she trying to make Grace feel left out on purpose? Grace had probably seen them looking at it at school, but they hadn't really told her about it. Should Kat explain to Grace what the Puppy Collection was or would Maya be angry?

"Maya," Kat said in a low voice. "Listen, about the Puppy Collection…"

Just then they reached the park. Murphy stuck his nose in the air and sniffed. He began pulling on the leash excitedly. Maya cried out, "Yahoo! Here we are. Let's run!"

"Yes, come on, Grace!" Kat cried, making a point of including her new friend. "Let's go!"

The three girls took off across the wide open field. Kat laughed as the puppy bounded happily alongside her on his dainty paws.

When they reached the playground on the other side, the girls stopped, panting and laughing. Grace bent down and patted the puppy.

"Good boy, Murphy!" said Grace. The puppy looked up at her with his brown eyes and wagged his tail.

"Doggy! Doggy!" A little girl was standing in the sandbox with several other toddlers, looking at Murphy. There were also several children on the slide and the swing set.

The little girl waved her red plastic shovel. She began to run toward them. "Doggy! Doggy!"

Murphy saw her coming and immediately crouched between Kat's legs.

"Want pet doggy! Want pet doggy!" the little girl cried.

Before she could get too close, the little girl's mother caught up to her and scooped her up. "No, honey. We have to ask before we pet a dog," the mother said firmly. "Is it all right?" she asked Kat. "Can my daughter pet your dog?"

"Murphy is nervous of new people," said Kat. "But it's okay to pet him. Just slowly put out your hand," she told the little girl, "and let him sniff it. Then you can stroke him gently."

"Like this," said the mother. She showed her daughter what to do, and then the little girl put out her hand for Murphy to sniff. Murphy was nervous at first. He put his head down low and cowered. But then, as the little girl waited patiently, he lifted his head and smelled her hand. He wagged his tail. But when she reached out to pet him, he pulled back, startled. His whole body was tense.

"It's okay, Murphy," said Kat. "They aren't going to hurt you."

The mother crouched down beside her daughter. She encouraged the little girl to hold out her hand again. Once more, Murphy sniffed the girl's hand. This time, when she slowly reached out to pet his back, Murphy wagged his tail happily.

"Tank you!" said the little girl. She gave a wave as she ran off back to the playground.

"Yes, thank you." The mother smiled and strode after her.

"Why are shelties so afraid of people?" Grace wondered.

"Don't worry. Einstein will tell us." Maya was teasing Kat. "Kat-Nip spends hours reading about dogs on the Internet. Her favorite book is *Dog Breeds of the World*. You've read it—what?—about twenty times?"

Kat shrugged. "I know. I'm hopeless," she admitted. Then she explained, "Some dogs are just a little more shy than others. Most shelties start out that way as puppies. They can be upset by noise or strangers. When they are shy or nervous, they might bark or run away.

It's important to socialize shelties when they're still young. We need to help this little guy get to know lots of strangers. He'll learn who he can trust and who is safe. He'll be happier!" said Kat.

"I've got an idea," Maya said. "What if we take turns holding Murphy's leash each afternoon? Then he'll get used to all of us. He'll learn to trust people."

"That makes sense," Kat agreed. She turned to Grace. "Here you go, Grace. It's your turn," Kat said.

Then she saw Maya frown.

 Grace's face lit up as she took the leash. "Okay, come here, Murphy," she said to the sheltie. She took a few steps. "Come with me."

But the puppy wouldn't budge. He stared up at her with sad eyes. He wouldn't move from between Kat's legs.

"Here's a stick. Let's throw it for Murphy to distract him," Maya suggested. "And we can use it to teach him to fetch and to come when we call." She waved the stick, showing it to Murphy. "Here we go! Ready, Murphy? Go get the stick!" She threw it a short distance.

Instantly the puppy sprang forward and ran to the stick. The leash was a retractable one so he could run far and still be safe. Murphy grabbed the stick between his teeth. He growled and wrestled with it. Then he tossed it in the air.

The girls laughed. "Such a fierce puppy!" teased Grace. "Okay, now come, Murphy," she called. "Come to me!"

Murphy looked at her, but he stayed where he was, chewing happily on the stick.

"Murphy, come!" Grace called again. "Come here!"

Now Murphy got up. But instead of coming to Grace, he grabbed the stick between his teeth and headed toward Kat. Grace pulled gently on the leash. "Here, Murphy!" she said again firmly. "Come to me, boy!"

When Murphy felt the pull on his collar, he stopped. He sat and looked at Grace. He looked back at Kat, and then at Grace again.

Maya clapped her hands together. "Oh, he is so adorable!"

"Come, Murphy. Good pup, come here!" Grace called encouragingly. She slapped her hand on her knees.

Murphy looked one more time at Kat, but then he headed toward Grace. When he reached the girl, he dropped onto her feet and resumed chewing the stick.

"Good boy, Murphy!" Grace said, patting Murphy's head.

"Way to go, Grace," said Maya, nodding.

Grace threw the stick for Murphy four more times. On the third and fourth try, the puppy came back to her without even glancing at Kat.

Then it was Maya's turn to hold the leash. Murphy was uncertain at first. He looked at Kat, at Grace, and then at Maya. But this time he adapted more quickly. On the second throw, he came straight to Maya when she called. He even wagged his tail when she praised him.

"Time for a break?" Kat asked. She pointed to the edge of the park. There was a hill with grassy slopes and a grove of trees on top. "Want to climb? There's a great view from there."

The hilltop was one of Kat's favorite places in the neighborhood. She liked to go there on weekends. Sometimes she sat looking out over the park and the town. Sometimes she walked around the woods on the top of the hill to the other side. She sat and looked out over the countryside. Wherever she was on the hilltop, she would dream about having her own puppy one day.

Maya handed the leash to Kat. "Your turn."

"Murphy? What about you, boy? Think you can make it all the way to that hill and up to the top?" Kat asked.

Murphy cocked his head. He wagged his tail. He smiled at Kat.

Kat laughed. "That's another trait of shelties," she pointed out. "I've read about it, and now I've seen it for myself. They really do smile!"

Grace laughed. "Yes, he's smiling!" she agreed.

"Okay, here we go!" Kat cried. "Come on, Murphy!"

The sheltie bounded forward and the girls followed. They ran all the way across the field to the hill. Then up they went, higher and higher.

When they reached the top, the girls flopped

down in the shade of the woods. Murphy lay beside Kat, panting. He licked her hand once, twice. She stroked his round belly.

"I like it up here," said Grace happily.

"Me too," agreed Maya.

"Grace, I can see your house from here," said Kat. "Maya, that's where Grace lives." She pointed to the street that bordered the park. "Grace, you're so lucky to live right beside the park."

"I wish we'd been able to stay on our farm,"

said Grace softly. "But since we couldn't, it is nice to live beside a park. Bella would have liked it."

Grace's family had recently moved to town so they could be closer to Grace's grandparents. Just before they moved, Grace's dog, Bella, had died.

Kat wanted to hear more about Bella, but Murphy jumped up. He turned toward the trees and barked. His puppy voice didn't sound very fierce, but he barked again and again.

"What's wrong, Murphy?" Kat stood up, holding tightly to Murphy's leash. He pulled hard. He kept barking. "Do you hear someone? Is someone there?"

"I don't see anyone," said Maya casually. She rolled onto her stomach. "I'm sure it's nothing."

"Murphy, calm down," said Kat firmly. She couldn't tell if the puppy was scared or excited. Maybe both.

"What should we do?" Grace had scrambled to her feet. She looked nervously into the woods. Her arms were straight at her sides. Her hands were tight fists. "What if someone's there? Once, when Bella and I were out..."

"Seriously, Grace?" Maya said. She laughed. "You're scared just because this sweet little guy is barking? Just calm down."

"First of all, I am calm." Grace frowned at Maya. "Second, sometimes dogs sense things we can't. They know when there's danger."

"Oh, you're the dog expert now, are you?" Maya said.

"No, but I did actually own a dog," Grace said defensively. "Did you?"

Maya glared at Grace. Then she shrugged. "Whatever."

Kat's heart was pounding. Her friends were fighting! Murphy was barking! What was going on?

CHAPTER 5

Well, if this is such a big deal, let's not just sit here," said Maya. "Come on. Let's find out what Murphy is worried about."

"Well, I'm not going in those woods," said Grace firmly. She crossed her arms.

"No kidding. I am so surprised," Maya said dryly. "Kat?"

Kat hesitated. She looked at Maya, and she looked at Grace. She felt caught in the middle.

But when Murphy whined and looked up

at her, Kat made up her mind. "We'll be right back, Grace," she said. "We'll be okay."

Kat let Murphy lead the way. She held the leash tightly, and she and Maya followed the puppy into the forest. There wasn't a path. They had to push their way through the tangled bushes and pine branches. It was difficult to walk. It was difficult to see.

But Murphy seemed to know where he was going. He was still pulling, but he had stopped barking. He was wagging his tail.

"What is it, Murphy?" Kat asked him again. "What are we looking for?"

They were almost through the small woods and out the other side.

Suddenly, the sheltie puppy stopped. He lay down, putting his chin on his paws.

"Puppies sometimes do that when they meet an older dog," said Kat. "But…"

"Look! Right under that tree!" cried Maya, pointing.

Kat looked at the pile of leaves and there, curled up tightly in a ball, was a tan cocker spaniel. She was whimpering sadly.

"It's a dog! Maybe it's lost," breathed Maya.

"Well done, Murphy! Good boy. You're a

hero!" said Kat, giving Murphy a quick pat on the back.

As the girls and Murphy hurried closer, the spaniel heard them. It sat up and faced them, wagging its tail. Its silky coat was long on its legs and body, almost touching the ground.

"Oh, look. It's an elderly dog. Its face is gray," said Kat. "You poor thing. How did you get lost?"

The spaniel looked at them with sad brown eyes. Its wide ears drooped.

"It's so sweet! I wonder how long it's been here," Maya exclaimed.

Slowly the spaniel got to its feet. It trotted stiffly straight up to Murphy and gave the puppy a friendly "thank you" lick on the nose. Murphy wagged his tail happily.

Maya crouched down. She put out her hand. "Come, come and say hi to me," Maya invited.

The spaniel smelled Maya's hand. Then it leaned against her leg while Maya gently rubbed its neck. "It's a cocker spaniel, right, Kat?"

"I think so," said Kat. "I think it's an American cocker spaniel, not an English cocker spaniel. American cockers are a little smaller. Their skulls are rounder and their muzzles are shorter."

"I wonder who it belongs to," Maya said. "It's not even wearing a collar! No tags, no address, no phone number." She looked into the cocker spaniel's brown eyes. "What's your name?" she asked. "Where did you come from?"

The elderly dog only wagged its tail.

"If it had come up the hill from the park side, we would have seen it," said Kat. "It must have climbed the hill on this side. Let's go right there, to the edge of the woods. Maybe we'll see someone at the bottom of the hill searching for the poor thing."

"Okay," said Maya. Then she spoke to the dog. "Would you mind if I picked you up?" Cautiously, Maya lifted the spaniel. It snuggled into her chest.

The girls walked the short distance and came out of the woods. There were only three streets at the bottom of the hill. Beyond, the town ended and the countryside began.

Right away, the spaniel gave a little woof. Murphy's ears tilted forward.

From far away came a woman's voice. "Tawny! Tawny! Where are you, Tawny?"

The spaniel gave a happy whine.

There, at the bottom of the hill, was a tall, thin elderly woman leaning on a cane. She peered around her, looking here and there.

"Are you Tawny?" Maya asked the dog. "Is that your owner?"

The cocker spaniel wiggled excitedly and yipped again.

"Tawny! Tawny!" the woman called, cupping her hand around her mouth. "Where are you, girl?"

"Should I set her down?" Maya asked Kat.

"Yes, I think so," Kat replied. "The dog seems to know this woman. She must belong to her."

Maya set down the squirming dog. It trotted down the hill as fast as it could go. "Yip! Yip!" it barked.

"Tawny, is that you?" the woman called. "You naughty girl! You come right here."

A few moments later, Tawny reached the bottom of the hill. She pressed herself against her owner's legs. She yipped again.

The girls waited for the woman to look up to see where Tawny had come from. They waited for the woman to wave a thank-you to them.

But she didn't.

Instead she reached into her pocket. Tawny sat down nicely, and the woman gave her a treat.

Still, the woman didn't look up the hill. She bent down and slipped a collar around Tawny's neck. She clipped on a leash. Then she slowly straightened up.

Now, finally, she looked up, right at Kat and Maya. Kat smiled and waved.

But the woman didn't wave. She didn't call out. She and the cocker spaniel headed away across the grass. Only Tawny looked back up the hill and gave a last good-bye wag of her tail.

CHAPTER 6

Kat frowned. "That wasn't very nice. We found that woman's dog and returned it to her. And she didn't say anything."

"Not even a wave," said Maya.

"Oh well." Kat shrugged it off. "At least Tawny is safe and sound now." She glanced at her watch. "It's almost five thirty. Already time to take Murphy back to Tails Up!"

Suddenly Kat remembered Grace, waiting for them on the other side of the woods. She glanced at Maya.

"Maya, what's going on with you and Grace? I know you don't know her very well, but you said you'd try to be her friend."

Maya shrugged. "I said I'd try, and I have. I didn't say it would work."

"Maya," Kat complained. "How can you

say you've tried? You've hardly spent any time with her!"

Maya shrugged again. "No, but sometimes… you just know about a person." She gave a little shake. "She just rubs me the wrong way."

Kat didn't know what to say, so the girls made their way back through the woods in silence. When they reached the other side, Kat stopped short. She looked around. She couldn't see Grace anywhere.

"Where is she? Where's Grace?" she asked. She shot Maya an angry look.

But just then Grace stood up. "I'm right here," she called out. She'd been sitting under a tree, waiting. "So what happened?"

Kat was relieved that Grace was still there and was being friendly.

She explained about Tawny as the three girls headed back to Tails Up! with Murphy. It was awkward. Maya didn't say a word to Grace the whole way. Grace didn't say a word to Maya.

"Good-bye, sweet little Murphy. And thanks again for helping us find the lost cocker spaniel!" Kat told the sheltie pup. She put him in his kennel and promised him that they'd be back tomorrow.

The girls walked together to Kat's house, which was just up the street from Tails Up! But before they went in, Grace took Kat aside. "Are you sure you still want me to come for dinner?" she asked.

"Of course. Why wouldn't I?" replied Kat. She wasn't sure what to do. So she pretended everything was okay, even though she knew Grace was feeling awkward with Maya.

"Hi, Katherine!" said Kat's mother when she heard the girls come in. She came hurrying out her home office. "Hi, Maya! And you must be Grace. It's very nice to meet you." She smiled at Kat's new friend. "I'm glad you're having dinner with us tonight!"

"Thanks. Me too," said Grace shyly.

"We'll be up in my room, Mom," said Kat. "You'll call us when it's time to set the table?"

"Count on it!"

The girls went up to Kat's bedroom. When Grace stepped inside, she caught her breath. The walls were covered in posters and pictures of puppies. The shelves of the bookcase were filled with books about puppies and even stuffed toy puppies.

Maya flopped down on the bed with her back to Grace. "Can you tell this girl is a tiny bit dog crazy?"

"What a great room!" Grace said. "I love it!" Then she made a face. "Oh, my mom told me to call when we got here. Can you show me where the phone is, Kat?"

"Sure. It's in our den." Kat took Grace down the hall and into the den and then returned to her room. She sat down and stared at Maya. "Listen, Maya," she said, "when we started our walk with Murphy, you mentioned the Puppy Collection. In front of Grace. But she doesn't really know about it yet."

"So?" Maya said. She rolled over onto her back. She plumped Kat's pillow under her head.

Kat hesitated. Maya wasn't making this easy.

"So, I want to tell her about it. I want her to help us with it."

Maya didn't say anything.

"What do you think? She loves puppies too. If she's going to be our friend, we should ask her to help us with our Puppy Collection," said Kat. There. She'd said it. She held her breath.

Maya frowned.

"Remember when you first met Grace? You didn't like her right away. Now, apparently, you do. Well, it's a lot to expect that I'll like her right away too. Besides, just because I said I'd try to be her friend, it doesn't mean she has to do everything with us." Maya sat up on the bed. "You asked me to help you at Tails Up! Then you asked her. Fine. You and I came up with the idea for the Puppy Collection. And now you want her to help with it too." Maya crossed her arms. "Well, maybe I don't want her to know about it."

The girls stared at each other in silence.

Grace came back into the room. Her face was stony. Her fists were clenched. She didn't look at Kat or Maya. "I have to go," she said in a low voice.

Kat jumped up. Oh no. Grace must have heard them talking. "But…"

"My mom changed her mind," Grace continued. "She wants me home for dinner."

Kat was sure they had hurt her feelings. "Grace…"

"I'm sorry, Kat," Grace said. Her eyes slid to Kat's and then away. "Maybe I can come another day."

"Grace, is that really true?" asked Kat. "Did your mom—"

Maya interrupted. "That's too bad," she told Grace. "See you tomorrow at school."

"Yeah. See you," Grace replied. "Bye, Kat," she added, and she left the bedroom, closing the door behind her.

 at glared at Maya. "That was not very nice," she said. "Grace is my friend."

"Oh, is she? Well, I thought I was your friend," Maya replied. She was still sitting on Kat's bed.

Kat blinked. "You know you're my friend. But Grace is too. And it wasn't very nice for you to…dismiss her like that."

Kat went to the bedroom door. "I'm going to go and say a real good-bye," she told Maya.

But as she left her room, she heard the front door close. Kat pounded down the stairs.

"I'll be right back, Mom," she called. She hurried out onto her front porch. Grace was running. She was halfway down the street.

"Grace! Wait!" she cried. But Grace must not have heard, because she kept running.

By the time Kat caught up to her friend, the girls were close to the park, more than halfway to Grace's house. Not only had Grace stopped running, but she'd even stopped walking.

"Grace! I'm sorry," Kat told her, trying to catch her breath.

Grace held up her hand. "Shhh… Listen."

The girls stood together, quiet.

Then, there it was—the sound of a dog whimpering.

"I hear it!" Kat said. "But where's it coming from? Where's the dog?"

"Over here, I think," Grace said.

Kat followed her across the street and into the park.

"Yip! Yip!" A cocker spaniel was walking slowly across the field. As the girls watched, she sat down to rest. She looked sad.

"I don't believe it. It's Tawny!" cried Maya.

Kat and Grace turned around in surprise. Maya was right there behind them.

Maya shrugged. "Well, I wasn't going to stay at your place all by myself," she said to Kat.

Kat frowned, but she turned her attention back to the cocker spaniel and Grace.

"This is the lost dog, Tawny," Kat told Grace. "The one Murphy found on the hill."

"Tawny, come here, girl," called Maya gently. "What are you doing here?" She crouched down and patted the dog's head. "Where's your owner this time?"

Kat looked up and down the street. There was no tall woman in a black dress anywhere in sight.

Maya scooped the dog up into her arms. Grace came to stand next to Maya. "Oh, she's so sad." Grace's voice was trembling. "Can I pet her?"

Maya didn't look at Grace. "Sure," she said.

"But what's happened? Why does she keep getting loose?" Kat said.

"At least she has her collar on this time," Maya pointed out.

Grace bent closer to Tawny, examining the cocker spaniel's collar. "Oh no. Looks like her tags have fallen off! She doesn't even have a registration tag on her collar, so we don't have any way of finding out where she lives." Grace frowned. "Her owner doesn't seem very responsible."

Maya shook her head. "No, she doesn't."

"Well, luckily we have an idea of where Tawny lives. Probably near the bottom of the hill where Tawny's owner stood calling her, right?" Kat suggested. "We should try to take her back there. We might be able to find the right house."

"I don't know about that." Grace put her hands on her hips. "Maybe this woman doesn't deserve to have a dog. She's lost her dog twice? That's terrible."

"You know, I actually agree with Grace," Maya said firmly. "Losing your dog twice in one day? Pretty sad."

"Having a dog is a privilege," said Grace. "I'd give anything to have my own dog back. And here's someone with a dog and she doesn't care that it's gone…"

"Yeah, we don't even know if we can find her. Maybe we shouldn't try," said Maya.

Grace nodded. "Yeah."

Kat was confused. Maya had treated Grace badly all day, so she was happy the two girls were finally agreeing on something. But not even try to find Tawny's owner? Kat wasn't sure she could agree with Maya and Grace on that.

Kat's thoughts tumbled and turned. If they didn't try to find the owner, maybe the three of them could keep Tawny. They could take turns. How could her parents say no to her looking after a lost dog?

Maybe. Or was Kat just being selfish?

It was exciting to think about having a dog. It was what Kat had always wanted. But when she thought about keeping Tawny, she felt excited and sad at the same time. It was like the feelings were wrestling inside her.

Kat reached down and petted Tawny. The little elderly cocker spaniel was now sitting, resting her legs. She looked like she was counting on the girls to do what was right.

Suddenly Kat knew. She'd been thinking of it all wrong. They had to put Tawny's needs first.

"Listen," she said. "We don't know anything about Tawny's owner. Tawny is lost, and she's sad. She needs to go home."

"But just because Tawny is sad, it doesn't mean her owner is taking good care of her," said Maya. "Maybe she's just really loyal."

"Some dogs put up with a lot from their owners and still love them," Grace pointed out.

"So, we'll try to find Tawny's home, and we'll do our best to check out her owner. We won't leave her there if we think she isn't safe," said Kat. "Agreed?"

Grace hesitated. She frowned as she considered Kat's suggestion. Then she nodded. "Agreed," she said.

"Yes, agreed. Okay, Kat," Maya said impatiently. Then she gave a dramatic sigh. "Kat-Nip is almost always right," Maya told Grace. "You'll have to get used to it. It's just one of the hardships of being her friend."

Grace grinned. "I'll try," she said.

Kat rolled her eyes, but she was relieved that the two girls were finally getting along.

"Okay, so we'll head over with Tawny to her neighborhood? Scout out the area?" Maya asked. As usual, with the decision made, Maya wanted to leap into action.

"Okay. But it might take a while," said Kat. "Tawny seems pretty lost."

"Hey, I know!" Grace's face lit up. "Why don't we get Murphy to help? He was so great at guiding you two to Tawny in the first place. Maybe he can help sniff out Tawny's home!"

"That is such a great idea," said Kat. "Let's take Tawny back to my house. I'll ask my mom, and we can call Aunt Jenn."

The girls hurried back to Kat's house with Tawny. Grace and Maya waited outside with Tawny while Kat went inside. In a moment, she was back. "Mom said she'll hold dinner until we're done, but she said to be careful." Kat made a face. "Mom always says that. And Aunt Jenn says we can borrow Murphy! She's putting his leash on for us right now. She said she had a leash for Tawny too. Let's go!"

The girls hurried to Tails Up! When they got there, Aunt Jenn was waiting outside with Murphy. As soon as the sheltie pup saw the girls and Tawny, he wagged his tail excitedly.

Tawny squirmed happily in Maya's arms. Maya put down the cocker spaniel so the dogs could greet each other.

"Here you go," Aunt Jenn said. She gave Murphy's leash to Kat. Then she handed her a pink leash. "For this little lost dog," she said, rubbing Tawny's head.

"Thanks, Aunt Jenn. You're the best!" Aunt Jenn was so kind, and she loved dogs so much. She always thought of everything. Kat wanted to be just like her when she grew up.

"I'll be here when you're done," Aunt Jenn said. "Good luck, girls. Good luck, Detective Murphy!"

"Thanks again, Aunt Jenn," Kat said. Then she turned to Maya, Grace, Tawny, and Murphy. "Okay, let's hit the streets, gang. We're off to find Tawny's owner!"

CHAPTER 8

The girls headed back up the street, into the park, and across the field to the hill. Murphy tumbled along beside Kat, his head held high, his eyes sparkling. He seemed to sense they were on a mission. Although she did not have the same energy as the puppy, Tawny kept up well. *Maybe she knows she's going home*, thought Kat.

They circled the bottom of the hill until they reached its far side. Now they were on the edge of their town. Several streets making up a small neighborhood sprawled before them.

"Okay, when we stood up there, on top of the hill, and looked down, we saw Tawny's owner standing right here," said Kat. "When Tawny ran down the hill to her, they left together in that direction." Kat pointed down the street, to the east. "Right, Maya?"

"Right. So we'll begin by going that way," Maya said. "When we get close to her home, maybe Tawny will signal us in some way."

The girls walked on, watching to see if the cocker spaniel showed any interest in any of the houses they passed. But she didn't. Tawny looked here and there, but she was mainly interested in watching the puppy. And no wonder! Murphy snapped at the yellow head of a dandelion on a lawn. He grabbed a stick and marched along happily with it between his teeth. He stared as a flock of sparrows set flight from a tree branch.

At the end of the street, Tawny slowed in front of a two-story brick home. There was a tricycle on the porch and a tire swing on the tree.

"Is this it, Tawny?" Maya asked excitedly. "Is this your house?"

Tawny sat down on the edge of the lawn. Then she lay down.

As Kat stood examining the house, Murphy nudged the cocker spaniel curiously with his nose. When the older dog didn't move, the puppy flopped down beside her, snuggled up, and closed his eyes.

The girls laughed.

"Maybe this isn't Tawny's house. Maybe both the dogs are just tired!" Kat said, giggling.

"Murphy's little puppy legs are probably exhausted," agreed Grace. "And Tawny has run around a lot today. She was in the park this afternoon, and then she walked halfway to Kat's house."

"Maybe, but I'll go and check anyway while the dogs rest up," said Maya. She strode toward the house.

Kat grinned admiringly. Maya was so confident!

Maya knocked on the door. A little girl opened it. They saw her look toward the cocker spaniel and the sheltie lying on her front lawn. Then she shook her head.

Maya came back. "Nope. Tawny's not their dog. The mom called out to me from the kitchen though. She said she's seen an older woman walking a cocker spaniel, but she doesn't know exactly where she lives."

"So we're on the right track at least," said Kat. "And there are only two more streets."

Now both Tawny and Murphy jumped up. The little rest seemed to have given them new energy. Tawny swept her tail from side to side. Murphy pulled at the leash, ready for action.

"Okay, let's go, dogs," said Maya.

Off they went down the street. They walked around the corner and turned up the next street.

All of a sudden, Murphy began sniffing. He pulled them along toward a white picket fence that surrounded a small red house. His ears perked up. He began wagging his tail. Sniff, sniff, sniff!

"Murphy seems to recognize this smell," said Grace.

Murphy began pulling Kat along the fence toward the front gate. It was standing open just enough to allow a small dog to push through.

"Look! The gate isn't closed properly. That's how Tawny got out!" said Maya.

"Her owner should make sure the gate is closed before she lets Tawny into the yard," said Grace firmly. "She isn't taking very good care of her dog."

"No, she isn't," said Maya, scowling.

The cocker spaniel was wagging her tail and pulling toward the house too. She seemed to know where she was.

Murphy sat by the gate, looking proud.

"Murphy, good pup! I think you've done it. I think you've found Tawny's home," said Kat. She bent down and smothered the sheltie in kisses. He wiggled happily.

"Well," said Maya, "I still don't know if we should take Tawny back. Not if her owner can't even keep her gate closed." She crossed her arms.

"Me too," agreed Grace.

For a moment, Kat wished they'd never tried to find Tawny's home. She wished they'd thought about it longer, maybe overnight. Wouldn't it have been nice to fall asleep with the cocker spaniel curled up at the foot of her bed? Wouldn't it have been nice to wake up in the morning with Tawny there with her?

She looked down at the dog. The cocker spaniel continued to pull excitedly on the leash. Kat shook off the feeling of regret. Bringing Tawny home was obviously the right thing to do. She knew it.

"Tawny definitely wants to go home," Kat pointed out. "And besides, we don't know the whole story. We haven't even met Tawny's owner yet. Maybe…maybe there's something we can do to make things better for Tawny."

Maya and Grace considered Kat's words. "Okay, that makes sense," Maya said. "Grace?" Grace nodded. "Maybe you're right," she said. The girls passed through the gate. Tawny was so excited she was almost pulling Grace down the path toward the house. Kat, last in line with Murphy, stopped to latch the gate behind them. But instead of walking on, Murphy whined and sat down.

"What's up, Murphy?" Kat asked. "What's wrong?" Kat looked back. The gate had swung open. Again Kat closed the gate and latched it. But now she realized that the latch was broken. It wouldn't hold for more than a second or so.

"You're so clever, Murphy," Kat said, reaching down to pat the puppy's head. "What a good boy!"

As Maya knocked on the front door, Kat told the girls about the latch.

"Well, why hasn't Tawny's owner taken the time to fix it?" Grace said, frustrated. "How much trouble could that be?"

"Exactly," agreed Maya.

The girls waited in silence for several minutes. Tawny whined expectantly. But there was no response.

"Maybe she's not home," said Grace.

Kat's heart began to thump. For a wonderful moment, she imagined taking Tawny back home for the night. Maybe they could even take her to the park with Murphy tomorrow after school!

Maya knocked again. Still, nothing.

"Guess we'll have to come back some other time," Grace said with a shrug.

"Well, good try, Murphy," Kat said to the

puppy. "You led us right here, but there's no one home!"

The girls turned to go. But Grace said, "Oh, look. Tawny won't leave!" The cocker spaniel sat a few steps from the door, staring at it, refusing to budge as Grace gently pulled on the leash.

"We know this is your home," Grace said to her, "but your owner's not here. You have to come with us."

Now Tawny lay down. She put her head on her front paws and whined.

Kat felt terrible. Tawny was desperate to be back in her own home. Kat was sorry she'd ever hoped Tawny's owner wouldn't be here. What were they going to do?

Suddenly Murphy's ears swiveled toward the

front door. He gave a little bark and wagged his tail.

"No, Murphy. There's no one there," Kat told him.

But then she heard the faint sound of a woman's voice. "Yes? Yes, I'm coming!"

All of a sudden the front door opened.

CHAPTER 9

A tall elderly woman was in the doorway. It was the same woman they had seen with Tawny that afternoon. Now she leaned on a cane. She peered this way and that.

"Tawny? Tawny, is that you?" the woman called.

Tawny danced about on the end of the leash, whining. Grace unclipped the leash, and the cocker spaniel lunged forward, pressing herself against the woman's legs.

"Oh, Tawny, it is you!" The woman bent

down to pet her dog. "I'm so sorry. You've been out here a long time. Of course you want to come back in now." She paused. "But you didn't knock on the door, did you, Tawny? Of course not. I was certain I'd heard knocking…" She stood up holding Tawny.

Kat called out, "That was us knocking!"

She and Maya and Murphy headed back down the walkway toward the front door. They stopped beside Grace. "My name is Katherine, Kat for short," Kat explained. "These are my friends Maya and Grace. And this is Murphy. He's a Shetland sheepdog puppy."

"Oh! I didn't see you girls there. Or your puppy. My eyes...well, they aren't what they used to be, that's for certain!" The woman smiled. "This is my cocker spaniel, Tawny." Tawny squirmed in her arms and barked. "Tawny, quiet! And I am Mrs. Borman, Ida Borman. How can I help you?"

"Well, we wanted to speak to you about Tawny," said Kat.

"Oh my goodness." The woman's face fell. "What has my little rascal done now?"

"It's all right," said Kat quickly. "We like Tawny. She's a very sweet and friendly dog."

The woman smiled. "But how do you know her?" she asked. "Have we met before?"

"Um, yes and no," Kat said. She hesitated, unsure how to go on.

Maya stepped forward. "We were on the hill in the park this afternoon and we…well, Murphy really…found Tawny in the middle of the woods. She was lost. We brought Tawny out to the edge of the woods. Then we heard you calling, and Tawny ran to you. We saw you head off down the street with her, so we guessed that you must live in this neighborhood."

"Oh my!" said Mrs. Borman. She clutched Tawny close to her.

"Then Tawny showed up near Kat's house about an hour ago, all by herself. It looked like she was lost again. So the three of us, and

Murphy, brought her over here, hoping we could find your house. And with Murphy's help, we did," Maya said.

"Murphy has been a hero, twice," said Grace softly. "Haven't you, Murphy?" She reached down and petted the puppy. He licked her hand.

"Well, good heavens!" Mrs. Borman shook her head again. "Thank you so much for bringing my Tawny back. I knew she ran away earlier, but I didn't know she was loose again just now. And just the day before yesterday, a neighbor found her and brought her back. And once last week as well."

Tears came to her eyes. "As you may realize," she said, "I don't see very well. My eyesight was never very good, but it has become worse in the last little while. I'm not completely blind, but my doctor told me I should consider getting a guide dog."

Suddenly Mrs. Borman chuckled. Brusquely, she wiped the tears away. "A guide dog! Can you imagine? How do you think my Tawny would like sharing me with another dog? She'd be jealous as all get-out!"

The girls laughed. Murphy wagged his tail.

"Well, I don't need a guide dog, but I must do something about Tawny. I want to keep her safe. If something ever happened to her, well…" Mrs. Borman shook her head. "But I don't know how she keeps getting out!"

Kat's heart melted. Mrs. Borman obviously loved her dog very much.

The girls exchanged a look. Kat could tell that Maya and Grace liked the woman too.

"Mrs. Borman," said Maya carefully, "we think that Tawny's getting out through the front gate. When we got here, it wasn't latched."

"Not latched? Well, that can't be. I latch it every time I let Tawny out in the yard alone. I always close the gate!" Mrs. Borman said.

"The gate closes, but the latch is broken, so the gate swings open again," explained Kat.

A look of surprise crossed the woman's face. "Oh dear," she said. "Thank you so much for letting me know. I am very grateful. As soon as I go in, I'll arrange to have the latch fixed. And I certainly won't let Tawny out loose in the yard until it is!"

Grace smiled. "That's good," she said.

Mrs. Borman put her hand on her chest. "Thank you so much, girls," she said. Then her expression changed. "But it's not enough," she said. She looked thoughtful. She frowned. "It's not really enough."

The girls looked at each other in surprise. Not enough?

"I wonder," said Mrs. Borman. Now the woman was standing up straighter. She wasn't even leaning on her cane. "I think I know something else that would help. Would you girls be able to do one more thing for me?"

"Yes," said Kat quickly. "What is it?"

"Would you be able to help me out by walking Tawny once in a while?" Mrs. Borman suggested.

Kat let out a squeal of happiness. Maya's eyes opened wide. Grace bit her lip.

"Could we?" Kat breathed. "Could we walk Tawny?"

"I would appreciate it," Mrs. Borman said. "That is, if you have time. I know you already have a dog of your own…"

"Oh no, Murphy isn't ours. We're just looking after him." Kat explained that her aunt's grooming salon also boarded dogs. She told Mrs. Borman that she, Maya, and Grace were helping out because they were crazy about dogs. "So we'd love to walk Tawny once in a while too," said Kat. "Right, Maya? Grace?"

"Right," the two girls answered as one.

Mrs. Borman held Tawny close.

"Oh my, thank you again, girls," she said. "Thank you from the both of us. And if I can ever help any of you, please do let me know."

CHAPTER 10

How did it go?" asked Aunt Jenn.

"Murphy was amazing. He actually helped us find Tawny's house!" said Kat. "Didn't you, puppy?" Kat scratched behind Murphy's ears, and he wagged his tail happily.

"That's wonderful!" said Aunt Jenn. "Well, it's getting late. You girls should head home for dinner. I'll take Murphy inside. You'll come and walk him again tomorrow after school?"

"We sure will," agreed Kat. She, Maya, and Grace said good-bye to Aunt Jenn. They headed up the street, chatting happily about their adventure.

When they got near the street that bordered the park, Grace suddenly stopped. "Well," she said uncertainly, gesturing toward the street. "My house is that way. I guess I'll see you tomorrow."

"Aren't you coming for dinner?" Kat asked. Then she remembered what had happened earlier. How Grace had overheard Maya talking about the Puppy Collection. Then Grace saying she had to go home for dinner.

"Listen, Grace," said Maya. "You should come. I'm sorry I've been rotten to you. It's just...hearing you talk about Bella, your dog...I was jealous. You've had a dog, and I'll probably never ever get one. Plus, I've never had to share my best friend before. It's not as easy as I thought. So I was mean to you." She bit her lip. Then she gave a half smile. "Plus, if you don't come with us, I may be forced to listen to Kat-Nip's jokes all by myself. No one should have to suffer through that alone."

Kat pretended to be offended. Then she turned and winked at Grace. Grace grinned.

"So, do you forgive me, Grace? You should. First, because I'm irresistible. And second, because if you do, you'll get to help us with our Puppy Collection, right, Kat?" Maya said.

Kat's eyes widened. Quickly, she nodded. "Yes! That's right!" she agreed.

"So, come on. What do you say?" Maya said, taking Grace's arm.

Grace blushed. "Well, okay," she agreed. "But, what exactly is the Puppy Collection?"

Kat and Maya explained it to Grace as they walked to Kat's house. And then, right after dinner, they hurried up to Kat's room to show Grace the scrapbook.

"This is Bailey," said Kat. She pointed to a photo of a yellow Labrador retriever pup.

"Look at his beautiful green eyes. He was the first puppy we looked after for Aunt Jenn. He was adorable."

"In our Puppy Collection, we put in a few photos or drawings of the puppy," explained Maya. "And a description too."

She read out Bailey's note: "*Bailey is a Labrador retriever puppy. He is eight weeks old. He is being housebroken, and he is doing well! Bailey likes to chase toys and shake them. He is very gentle. He likes to give us kisses.*"

"And here's Riley. You remember her from the park last week, right?" said Kat.

"Oh, what a great photo of her. She was so sweet!" said Grace.

"And this is a picture that Kat drew of her," said Maya.

Kat didn't like showing people her drawings. She didn't think she was a good artist, and she worried others would laugh. But Grace didn't.

"She has dark-brown eyes just like that," said Grace admiringly.

Maya read out the description of Riley: "*Riley is a three-month-old golden retriever. She likes to bark at ants! She is learning to sit, lie down, and come. She has a beautiful puppy smell.*"

"Hey, I know you both have to go home soon," said Kat. "But let's make some notes about Murphy."

"Great idea!" agreed Maya. "And I'll bring my camera tomorrow and take a photo of him."

"And maybe you can do a drawing of him, Kat," Grace suggested.

Kat grinned. "Sure," she said.

"But first, there is something much, much more important that needs to be done," Maya announced dramatically.

The two girls looked at her blankly.

"Kat, comedienne extraordinaire? You must tell us a joke," said Maya. "How can we go on without a Kat-Nip joke?"

Grace clapped. "Of course! Yes, Kat, a joke! We need a joke!"

Kat stuck out her tongue at her friends. "If you insist." She thought for a moment, then she said, "What do dogs have that no other animals have?"

Maya and Grace looked at each other. They shook their heads. "Don't know," Maya said. "What?"

"Are you ready for this?" Kat asked. "Hold your sides. Okay, what do dogs have that no other animals have? Puppies!"

It was hard to tell who groaned louder, Grace or Maya.

"You asked for it!" Kat told them, shaking her finger at them.

"We sure did," Maya agreed, throwing herself on Kat's bed and pretending to roll around in pain. "But we never imagined it could be as bad as that, did we, Grace?"

"Never," said Grace, trying to hide her giggles. "Never!"

Kat sat and smiled, watching her two friends. It was a perfect ending to the day. Just perfect.

ABOUT THE AUTHOR

Award-winning author Susan Hughes has written over thirty books—both fiction and nonfiction—for children of all ages, including *Earth to Audrey, Island Horse, Four Seasons of Patrick, Off to Class: Incredible and Unusual Schools around the World,* and *Case Closed? Nine Mysteries Unlocked by Modern Science.* She is also a freelance editor and writing coach. Susan lives with her family in Toronto, Canada, in a house with a big red door—and wishes it could always be summer. You can visit her at susanhughes.ca.

Kat and Maya's
PUPPY ADVENTURES
continue with
BIJOU,
a shy bichon frise
puppy!

EVERY PUPPY NEEDS A FRIEND

PUPPY PALS

Bijou

SUSAN HUGHES

WATCH OUT FOR MORE PUPPY
PALS BOOKS FEATURING MANY
OTHER ADORABLE PUPPIES!

Kat giggles. *There are puppies everywhere! Some are tumbling in the grass. Some are chasing butterflies. Some are playing in the flower beds.*

Some puppies are white, some are brown, some are red with spots. There are dachshunds and Afghans. There are Boston terriers and cocker spaniels.

There are too many puppies to count!

"Hey, Kat!" a voice said. "It's for you."

"Hey, Kat!" her brother Aidan says. "They're for you, Sis. Any puppy you want. Mom and Dad

have finally agreed." He punches her gently on the shoulder.

Kat grins. She can't believe it! It's a dream come true.

But which one should she pick? The sweet black-and-white border collie with the sparkling eyes? The Bernese mountain dog pup wagging its rolypoly body? The cute Labrador retriever with the white star on its black tummy?

"Hey, Kat!" It was her brother's voice again. "Sis!"

Kat was sitting at the computer in the living room. It was Saturday. Kat had been looking at photos of different breeds of puppies on the computer until she began daydreaming.

"Earth to Kat," her brother said, handing the phone to her. "It's for you. It's Aunt Jenn."

Kat's favorite daydream in the world ended.

In real life she wasn't allowed to get a puppy.

Her parents said they didn't have enough time to look after puppies.

But she was happy her aunt was phoning her. Aunt Jenn was the best. She loved dogs as much as Kat did. She had opened up a dog-grooming salon in town. Her business was called Tails Up! Boarding and Grooming, and it was doing really well—better than she had thought it would. In fact, Aunt Jenn had just hired someone to help answer the phone and make appointments. But even with her new office helper, Aunt Jenn was still busy, busy, busy. So she often asked Kat to give her a hand. Most times Kat got her best friend, Maya, and her new friend, Grace, to come along. They usually helped Aunt Jenn with puppies that were boarding at Tails Up!

Kat grabbed the phone from Aidan. "Hi, Aunt Jenn!" she said.

"Hi, Kitty-Kat," said Aunt Jenn, using her special name for Kat. "Listen, I wonder if you can help me out. Things are usually busy here on Saturdays. But this morning, there is an extra challenge."

"Sure," said Kat. "What is it? Has someone left a puppy to board with you? Does he need a walk or a play in the yard?"

"Well, something like that—times three!" Aunt Jenn laughed. "This morning I came downstairs to the salon early to prepare for another day of business. I opened the main door to pick up the newspaper, and what did I find? A big cardboard box—with three little white bichon frise puppies in it!" Aunt Jenn said. Now her voice sounded a bit upset.

Kat gasped. "Three abandoned puppies?"

"Yes," Aunt Jenn said. She sighed. "I think they are about eight weeks old. I put them in a kennel in the doggy day care room, and I gave them food and water. They need more attention, but I'm so busy today. It's almost noon, and this is the first chance I've even had to call you. You don't mind helping out this afternoon?"

"Of course not!" Kat said quickly. "Is it okay if Maya and Grace come? We all love helping out at Tails Up! You know how dog crazy we are!"

"That would be wonderful," Aunt Jenn said. "That way there would be three of them and three of you!"

"I'll check with Mom and Dad," said Kat. "Then I'll call Maya and Grace."

"Oh, and Kitty-Kat, can you bring along poster-making supplies? It would be great if you could make posters advertising that the three pups need homes," suggested Aunt Jenn.

"Sure thing," said Kat. "See you in a flash. Or sooner!"